For Deborah, Isobel and Tom—DB

For Kippy, Ollie & Jess
I love the way you love me—AJ

Little Hare Books
4/21 Mary Street, Surry Hills
NSW 2010 AUSTRALIA

National Library of Australia Cataloguing-in-Publication
Bedford, David, 1969- .
    The way I love you.

    For children.
    ISBN 1 877003 49 2.

    1. Dogs - Juvenile fiction. I. James, Ann. II. Title.

    823.92

Designed by Louise McGeachie
Produced by Phoenix Offset, Hong Kong
Printed in China
5 4 3 2 1

The way i love you

David Bedford & Ann James

LITTLE HARE

I love…

the way we
play our
games,

the way you run so fast,

the way you
come straight
back.

That's the way I love you.

I love…

the way we
always share,

the way you're
my best friend,

the way we
both pretend.

That's the way I love you.

I love…

the way you tell me things,

the way you
jump so high,

the way you
smile your
smile.

That's the way I love you.

I love…

the way you
understand,

the way you show me how,

the way we are
right now.

That's the way I love you.

I love…

the way you always care,

the way you're always there,

that's the way I love you.

That's the way I love you.